A VERY GRUMPY CHRISTMAS

WOLF VALLEY: A VERY GRUMPY HOLIDAY
BOOK 4

SHAW HART

Copyright © 2024 by Shaw Hart

www.shawhart.com

All rights reserved.

No part of this publication may be reproduced, transmitted, downloaded, distributed, stored in or introduced into any information storage or retrieval system, in any form or by any means, whether electronic, photocopying, mechanical or otherwise, without express permission of the publisher, except by a reviewer who may quote brief passages for review purposes. This book is a work of fiction. Names, characters, places, story lines and incidents are the product of the author's imagination or are used fictitiously. Any resemblances to actual persons, living or dead, events, locales or any events or occurrences are purely coincidental.

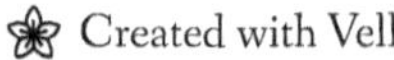 Created with Vellum

WANT A FREE BOOK?

***You can grab Sweets* Here.**
**Check out my website, www.shawhart.com for
more free books!**

*

I have a secret admirer...

Ginger:

When I got the first letter from my secret admirer, I was flattered.

With the second, I grew intrigued.

By the third, I'm starting to fall in love with him.

I wish that I could meet him in person, but I don't know how to arrange that.

Kip:

I've wanted Ginger Baker since the moment that I saw her.

She's so beautiful, so full of light.

I need that in my life, but I know that she would never be interested in me.

So, I do the only thing that I can to be close to her and start writing her letters.

When she writes back, demanding to meet, I know that I have a choice to make.

I can do as she asks and meet her under the mistletoe at the town party, or I can stay in the shadows, loving Ginger from a distance.

ONE

Kip

I LINGER in the shadows of the parking lot, waiting for her to come out and feeling like a creepy stalker.

Well, I mean, I guess I kind of am a stalker.

Shit.

Only hers, though. I've never done anything like this before, never wanted to. Not until I saw her.

Ginger Baker.

She moved to town with her sisters about a year ago, and I've been watching her ever since, trying to learn everything that I can about her. It's become an obsession, a compulsion. My feelings for her are out of control.

I'd like to say that it started as a mild interest, but the truth is that I've been obsessed with my curvy girl since the moment that she stepped foot in this town. It's why I've been doing crazy things, things that I never would have done in the past. Things like following her around and leaving notes for the last few months.

The sun is dipping below the horizon, painting the sky in swirls of orange and pink, but I'm not paying attention to the view. My focus is on Ginger. It's always on her.

I just need to get my daily dose of her, just one glimpse. That's why I'm out here, freezing my ass off.

Over the last year, I've learned a lot. I've learned that she's everything I'm not. She's bright, open, and full of life. Every time I see her, it feels like my chest tightens just a little bit more. She has my heart in a vise grip and doesn't even know it.

I've wanted to talk to her, *really* talk to her, for months now, to say something—anything—but every time I get close to her, the words get stuck in my throat, and I end up nodding or grunting at her like an asshole. And that scar on my face feels like it burns, reminding me of why someone like her would never want someone like me.

But I couldn't stay away from her, not for long. I had to get close, to bask in her light, to hear her infectious laugh. So, I did what any lovesick fool would do, and I started writing her secret love notes.

The first note was simple. I wrote that I loved seeing her smile, that her laugh was my favorite sound, and that I couldn't stop thinking about her. Then I left it on the windshield of her car, hoping it would make her smile.

And it had.

Now, it's been three months of me leaving letters, of pouring out my heart without ever signing my name. She's kept every note. I've seen them tucked into the pocket of her bag and coat, seen her rereading them sometimes when she's at work and it's slow. It's a small miracle, watching her read the words I'm too much of a coward to say out loud.

Tonight, there's another note, the same stationery as all of the others, carefully folded and placed under her windshield wiper. I stand far enough away that she won't notice me, my heart racing like a teenager waiting for his crush to notice him. It's pathetic, really. *I'm* pathetic. But when she walks out of Shelf Indulgence, her sister's bookstore, her dark red hair catching the last bit of daylight, all I can do is watch and hope she likes what I've written this time.

My eyes drink her in greedily, and I can't look away from her as she heads over to her old beat-up car.

I hate that damn thing. I've lost track of the number of hours that I've spent leaning over the hood, fixing the radiator and then the alternator, and then the spark plugs. The damn thing has been on its last leg for way too long, and she needs to replace it. For whatever reason, she refuses to, though, so I spend half of my nights making sure that it runs and my girl doesn't get stranded somewhere.

She reaches her car and spots the note almost instantly. She smiles, and it's like the whole world comes grinding to a halt. Her smile is the kind that makes you forget everything else. The kind that feels like warmth on a cold winter day. I watch as she takes the letter, her fingers brushing the edge of the paper as she opens it carefully, like she's afraid to damage it, like my note is something precious to her.

My breath hitches as she starts reading. I don't know why it still surprises me that she reads them so quickly, so eagerly. Or why I get so nervous as I watch her.

By the time she's finished, her smile has softened into something sweeter, something I wish was meant just for me.

"Are you stalking her again, Kip?"

I jump, startled, and glance to my right to find my best friend, Huxley, standing next to me, his arms crossed and a knowing smirk tugging at his lips.

"Not stalking," I lie, keeping my eyes on Ginger as she climbs into her car. She's still holding the letter as she starts the engine, and I can't help but feel a flicker of pride, or maybe it's hope.

"Sure," Huxley says with a shrug. "That's why you've been standing out here in the freezing cold for the last half an hour. Who doesn't love being outside when it's negative ten?"

"Exactly. I love it. It's... bracing."

He laughs, and I sigh. He's right, it's cold as fuck out here, and I'm pretty miserable. Seeing Ginger, though, makes it worth it.

"You could always try to watch her from indoors, ya know," he says.

I shoot him a glare, but he just chuckles. Huxley's been my best friend since birth, pretty much. We grew up together, graduated, and both joined the Marines. When I was shot and blown up last year and got out, he did too and joined me here in Wolf Valley. Now we own and run our own tourist helicopter business here in town called Semper Fly.

Huxley is the only one who knows how I feel about Ginger and about my letters to her. He's also the only one who doesn't think it's completely insane. At least, not most of the time.

"You know, you could just talk to her like a normal person," he suggests, his tone light but laced with a hint of seriousness. "Instead of... this."

"She wouldn't be interested," I say automatically, the words bitter on my tongue.

Huxley raises an eyebrow. "How would you know? You haven't even tried."

I don't answer. Instead, I watch as Ginger's taillights disappear down the road, a heavy sigh escaping my lips and coming out in a puff of white air. It's not that I don't want to talk to her. It's just... complicated. When I first moved to Wolf Valley after getting out of the military, I didn't expect much. I figured that I would move to a small town and try to blend in. I would do my best to enjoy a slow, quiet, lonely life.

Then I saw her and the way she lights up a room without even trying, the way she treats everyone like they matter. She was everything I needed but didn't think I deserved. Still don't.

"Man, you've got to do something," Huxley says, nudging me. "I can't keep watching you pine after her. It's getting nauseating."

I flip him off as I turn to head to my own truck, and he falls into step beside me.

"It's Christmas soon and then a new year. You gonna be that creepy guy leaving notes forever? Or are you actually going to tell her how you feel?"

"She's happy," I say, ignoring the sting in my chest. "She's fine without me. Besides, it's better this way."

"Better for who? You, hiding in the shadows, freezing to death? Or her, thinking she's falling for some fantasy dude who doesn't even exist?"

His words hit harder than I expect, and I clench my jaw. "I'm not some fantasy," I snap, but even as I say it, I don't fully believe it. Huxley's right. The person she's falling for isn't the real me. It's the version of myself I wish I could be. The guy who isn't broken or scarred, who isn't weighed down by his past.

But that's not who I am. Not anymore.

"Look, all I'm saying is, you've got to stop playing this game," Huxley says, his voice softening. "If you like her, really like her, then tell her. Don't let this secret admirer thing blow up in your face."

I stay silent, staring at the empty spot where Ginger's car was just moments ago. Huxley's right, but that doesn't make it any easier. If I tell her the truth, if I show her who I really am... what then? What if she looks at me the way I've always feared she would? With pity, or worse, disgust?

I've been hiding behind these letters because they're safe. It's easy to be confident on paper, to say all the things I could never say to her face. But sooner or later, I'm going to have to face the reality that I can't stay invisible forever. Not if I want a chance with her.

"She's going to the Christmas party," Huxley adds, almost as if reading my mind. "You know, the one she's been volunteering for and setting up?" He says, twirling his finger around us at all of the decorations.

I groan. Of course, he would bring that up. Every year, the town throws a huge holiday festival, complete with an insane amount of decorations and an obnoxious amount of mistletoe. It's supposed to be festive and light-hearted or whatever, but all I can think about is how impossible it would be to blend into the background at a place like that.

"So?" I ask, even though I already know where this conversation is headed.

"So, what happens if she stands under the mistletoe with someone else? What happens if she kisses someone else? Are you going to be okay with that?"

"Fuck no. She won't do that," I argue, and he gives me a skeptical look.

"You sure about that? She seems like she loves Christmas. I bet she would, even if it was just for the whole festive tradition."

"So, I'll stop her."

"How?"

"I don't know," I snap. "I'll figure it out.

"You going to shoot any guy who comes near her?" He asks, referencing the fact that we were snipers in the Marines. I don't bother to respond to that, mainly because the thought has crossed my mind before, and I know that if I answer, Huxley will be able to tell.

"Or," Huxley says with a grin, "this could be your chance. Show up. Talk to her. Maybe even be the one to kiss her under the mistletoe."

I shake my head. "You make it sound so simple."

"Because it is," he insists. "Look, I know you're scared, but you can't keep hiding. If you want something to happen, you've got to put yourself out there. Otherwise, you're just going to spend the rest of your life wondering what could've been."

I roll my eyes, but his words sink in deeper than I'd like to admit. Huxley's always been the fearless one, the guy who dives headfirst into everything without thinking twice. I used to be like that, too, once upon a time. But that was before the attack, before everything fell apart.

Now, I'm just a guy who writes letters to a girl who doesn't even know I exist.

But maybe... maybe I could change that.

"I'll think about it," I finally say, my voice barely above a whisper.

Huxley claps me on the back, his grin widening. "That's all I'm asking, man. Just think about it. You never know—Christmas miracles and all that."

I huff out a laugh, but the knot in my chest tightens all the same. The idea of actually talking to Ginger, of seeing the look on her face when she realizes who's been writing to her all this time—it's terrifying. But it's also tempting.

What if, just once, I let myself believe that she might want me too?

As Huxley rambles on about some plan to get me to the party, I glance down the road, imagining Ginger's face as she reads my next letter. It's a fantasy, I know that. But maybe it's time to stop hiding behind words and start living in the real world.

I'll talk to her, I decide, straightening my shoulders as we walk over to my truck.

Eventually...

TWO

Ginger

I WASN'T SUPPOSED to be the one getting the letter. That's what I told myself when I found the first one.

It was a cold, rainy day in early September and I'd had one of those mornings where everything seemed to go wrong, the kind of day that makes you question why you even bothered getting out of bed that morning.

I was late opening the bookstore, spilled coffee on my favorite sweater, and locked my keys inside the car. I had to walk back to my apartment to grab the spare and when I got back, that was when I found it.

I almost didn't see the letter tucked under my windshield wiper at first. I was rushing, trying to get back inside before the rain drenched me any more than it already had, but there it was—a folded piece of paper neatly placed under the wiper, its edges curling slightly from the damp air and drizzle.

I remember frowning, wondering if I had gotten a ticket

or something, but then I opened it and saw that it was on stationery. Stark white with a heart with an arrow on it in the bottom left corner.

My first thought when I realized that it was a love note, was that it had been meant for someone else. Wolf Valley was small, but we weren't immune to mistakes, and I figured someone had left it for the wrong person, that my car was common, and they had put it on the wrong windshield.

The words in the note were simple and kind. There was no name, no signature, just an anonymous message that made my heart race and my palms sweat for reasons I couldn't quite explain.

But instead of feeling flattered, I felt confused. I almost left a note of my own, telling whoever it was that they had the wrong person. I didn't get anonymous love letters. That sort of thing happened in romance novels, not real life. And certainly not to me.

Yet, for reasons I still don't fully understand, I didn't leave a note. I tucked the letter into my bag, and that was that. A fluke, I told myself. Just some strange, one-off occurrence.

Then came the second letter.

I decided to leave that letter on my car and write my own note, explaining that it was my car and they must have the wrong person.

Then I got the third note, that one addressed to me, and I realized that it wasn't a mistake. The letters were meant for me. There was no denying it anymore—I had a secret admirer.

It showed up a week later, tucked into the door of the bookstore this time. The stationery and handwriting were the same—careful, deliberate—but the words were different. This one was more personal, like whoever was writing to me knew me a little better now. They complimented me and told me that they used to love the color blue, but after seeing my eyes, it had changed to green.

By the time I read the fourth letter, I was hooked and starting to fall for him. Hard.

It's funny how quickly your perspective can shift. One moment, I was convinced the letters weren't meant for me, and the next, I was eagerly waiting for the next one, wondering what my mystery man would say. Every time I got a new one, it felt like a piece of a puzzle falling into place. I was dying to solve it and figure out who my secret admirer was. To tell him that I was obsessed with him too.

But there was a problem.

There was no pattern to the letters. Sometimes they'd show up at the bookstore or the bakery, whichever one of my sister's businesses I was working at that day. Other times they were slipped under my welcome mat at home, or on my car, and once, even slipped into my mailbox. They came at different times, on different days, with no rhyme or reason. I never knew when the next one would appear, and it was driving me crazy.

I needed to know who he was. I needed to figure out who the man that I was in love with was.

"Maybe it's the new guy in town," Cora says, leaning across my little kitchen table, her eyes twinkling with amusement as I tell her about the latest letter. "You know, Huxley? He's always looking at you."

I snort, shaking my head. "Huxley isn't looking at me, Cora. He's looking at you."

She laughs, the sound bright and full of mischief. "No, he's not."

I don't bother to correct her. Cora is sure that no one wants her, and I know that if I point out that he can't take his eyes off her, she'll just argue with me. Huxley is for sure in love with her, but he'll have to be the one to convince her of that.

Cora and I have been friends ever since she moved to Wolf Valley a few months after my sisters and I did. We became fast friends and hang out at least once a week. She's one of the only people here, besides my sisters, who know about the letters.

"I just wish I knew who he was," I admit, leaning back against the kitchen counter. "It's been months, Cora. Months of these letters and still no clue."

"Well," Cora says thoughtfully, tapping her chin, "there's got to be some kind of pattern, right? Have you noticed anything? Does he say anything that might give him away?"

I shake my head, pulling the most recent letter from my pocket and handing it to her. She unfolds it carefully, her eyes scanning the familiar handwriting as I watch her face for any sign of recognition.

"'Your smile is like sunshine on a rainy day,'" she reads aloud, her voice softening as she reaches the end. "'I hope one day I'll be brave enough to tell you this in person, but until then, I'll keep admiring you from afar.'"

Cora looks up at me, her eyes wide with excitement. "Ginger, this is so romantic! It's like you're living in a freaking romance novel!"

I chuckle, but my heart clenches in my chest. "Yeah, except in romance novels, the guy usually reveals himself by now."

"Well, maybe he's shy," Cora suggests, folding the letter and handing it back to me. "Or maybe he's waiting for the perfect moment."

I tuck the letter back into my pocket, biting my lip. "I

don't know, Cora. You don't think that if he wanted to, he would have said something by now? What if he never reveals himself? What if I'm just stuck here, reading these letters and wondering who he is for the rest of my life?"

Cora taps her fingers against the counter, her expression thoughtful. "Well, who do you think it could be? I mean, someone's got to be writing these letters. Let's make a list."

I laugh, shaking my head. "A list?"

"Yeah! A list of possible suspects," she says, her eyes gleaming with excitement. "Come on, it'll be fun."

I groan, but I can't help but smile at her enthusiasm. "Fine, but you're not going to find anything. I don't have a clue who it could be."

Cora pulls out a notepad from her purse and grabs a pen, poised to start writing. "Okay, first up: Huxley."

I roll my eyes again. "We already covered this. He's not interested in me."

"Okay, fine. What about his friend? Kip?"

My heart skips a beat at the mention of his name, and I quickly look away, pretending to rearrange the books on the counter.

Kip. The one person I'd been trying not to think about in connection to these letters.

"Why would you say Kip?" I ask, keeping my voice as casual as possible.

Cora gives me a knowing look. "Oh, I don't know. Maybe because you blush every time you hear his name?"

I feel the heat rise to my cheeks, and I curse my fair complexion. "I do not."

"Sure, you don't," she says, smirking. "But come on, Ginger. He's quiet, he keeps to himself, and he's always hanging around, but never too close. Sounds like secret admirer material to me."

I bite my lip, trying to ignore the way my heart flutters at the thought of Kip being the one behind the letters. The truth is, I've had a crush on Kip for as long as I can remember. Ever since I first saw him, there's been something about him that's drawn me in—something quiet, almost mysterious. But I never thought he'd be interested in me. Not really.

"Even if it is Kip," I say, trying to keep my voice steady, "why would he write me letters instead of just talking to me? He knows where I work. He could come in anytime."

"Shy, remember?" Cora asks and I sigh. "Or maybe he's scared. Or... I don't know. I mean, I barely know the guy. He keeps to himself."

I nod, my heart aching a little at the thought. I don't know much about Kip's past, but I've heard enough to know that he's been hurt. The scar on his face is a constant reminder of whatever happened to him, and I can only imagine the toll it's taken.

But could he really be the one writing me letters? Could Kip, the quiet, reserved guy who barely says more than a few words at a time, really be my secret admirer?

The thought sends a thrill through me, and I can't help the small smile that tugs at my lips.

"Okay, maybe it's Kip," I admit, glancing at Cora. "Or maybe I just want it to be him. But, how do I find out for sure?"

Cora grins, leaning forward with a gleam in her eye. "Leave him a note. Ask him to meet you. If it's him, he'll show up."

I bite my lip, considering the idea. It's risky. What if it's not him? What if I'm wrong, and I end up embarrassing myself? But at the same time, the idea of finally knowing the truth, of finally meeting my secret admirer face-to-face, is too tempting to resist.

"I'll think about it," I say.

"You'd better," Cora says with a wink. I laugh, shaking my head as I grab a few more books from the counter, trying to distract myself from the swirling thoughts in my head. Holiday magic, sure. But real life isn't a romance novel. Magic doesn't just happen, not without some effort. And writing a note? Asking Kip—or whoever this mystery man was—to meet me? That felt like a lot more effort than I was ready for.

Still, the idea buzzes in the back of my mind, refusing to let go.

"Are you helping out with the festival?" She asks me and I sigh.

"No, my car was making a weird sound last night and wouldn't start. I was going to try to take a look before I bring it over to the mechanics."

"You know how to fix cars?" She asks and I shake my head.

"Nope, no clue, but I want to at least try before I pay for someone else to do it. What if it's an easy fix?"

"Alright, let's go. I'll try to help."

She pulls her phone out as we head outside to where my old car is sitting.

"Uh, try to start it now?" She asks, already googling car starter issues.

I climb behind the wheel and send up a silent prayer as I stick the key in the ignition and turn.

"What the—" I mumble as my car starts right up.

"Sounds fine to me," Cora says, poking her head into the driver's side door.

"Yeah, that's so weird. It wouldn't start yesterday, and I

tried a bunch. This car is so old that before I moved here, I was bringing it in for work like at least once a month. Ever since, though, it's been running great."

"Maybe you should sell it or trade it in before it breaks for good," she suggests.

"It was my mom's," I whisper, and she nods, her eyes softening.

I turn the car off and climb out, locking the door behind me.

"I need to check in with Saffron," I tell her, and she nods, following me over to the bookstore and inside.

We both try to warm up a bit as I look around for my sister.

"We should talk about the holiday festival," Cora says, straightening up from the counter.

"Yeah, did you come up with any new ideas?" I ask her.

"Not really," she admits with a sigh.

"What are you two scheming about now?" My sister, Saffron, asks as she sweeps into the bookstore, her arms full of decorations.

Saffron owns the bookstore and I cover for her whenever she needs it. I do the same for my other sisters, Olive and Maple at their businesses. I'm the youngest of us and the only one who has no idea what she wants to do with her life.

As soon as we moved here, Olive, the oldest, opened her own bakery. She's always loved to cook so it made sense. Maple opened up her own adult toy store here in town and Saffron quickly followed with the bookstore. I was last, and so far, I've just been happy to help them out and hang out in town.

"Just trying to figure out who Ginger's secret admirer is," Cora says with a mischievous grin.

"Oh, please." Saffron rolls her eyes as she sets down a box of garlands. "That's easy. It's Kip."

I nearly drop the stack of books I'm holding, my heart thudding painfully in my chest. "Why does everyone think it's Kip?"

"Because it's obvious," Saffron says with a shrug, as if it's the most natural conclusion in the world. "He's been into you since the day he moved here, but he's too shy to make a move. The letters? Classic move from someone who's too nervous to talk to you in person."

I gape at her, feeling a blush creep up my neck. "That's ridiculous. If Kip liked me, he would've said something by now."

Saffron arches an eyebrow, giving me a look that's somewhere between amusement and disbelief. "Ginger, he's practically in here every day. Don't you think it's a little suspicious that he always finds a reason to hang around?"

I open my mouth to argue, but the words die on my lips. I can't deny that Kip is always around, always hovering in the background but never quite stepping into the spotlight. He's quiet, yes, but there's something else, something deeper. Maybe I've been too wrapped up in the mystery of the letters to see what's been right in front of me all along.

"Maybe he just likes reading," I argue, and Saffron snorts.

"*I* love reading, and even I'm not reading a book a day like he is. He's always buying books. Since you started helping out here more, he's become my best customer, and when I talked to Olive, she said the same thing. He's even asked what pastries you worked on, and he only buys those whenever you help out at the bakery."

Cora snickers, clearly enjoying my discomfort. "See? Even Saffron agrees. It's Kip."

I huff, crossing my arms. "I still think it could be someone else."

"Like who?" Saffron asks, tilting her head. "Name one other person who's shown even a fraction of the interest in you that Kip has."

I frown, feeling cornered. "I don't know. Maybe it is Kip. But what if it's not?"

"Then you'll never know unless you ask," Cora chimes in. "Come on, Ginger. What have you got to lose?"

I sigh, glancing between my sister and my best friend. They both look at me with such confidence, as if it's already decided—Kip is the one, and all I have to do is ask him to meet me. But the truth is, I'm scared. Scared of being wrong, scared of getting my hopes up, scared of getting hurt. Scared of what it means if Kip really is the one behind the letters.

"I'll think about it," I mutter, though I can tell by the way they're grinning that they don't believe me for a second.

"Don't think too long," Saffron says, grabbing the decorations again. "I'm going to start decorating for Christmas. Unless... you want to do it."

She gives me a teasing smirk. It's well-known in my family that I love Christmas. There's just something about that time of year that makes me happy. I've had my apartment decorated for weeks, and my tree has been up since the middle of November.

"You know I want to," I grumble, snatching the box of decorations out of her hands.

I hear her and Cora laugh as I head over to the front windows and get to work. I smile as I go, and my mind drifts back to Kip.

I wonder if he'll be at the holiday festival next week. He

hasn't really gone to any of the other town events, but maybe this time will be different.

Cora and I have volunteered to help set up, and I need to finish up here quickly so that we can head over to town hall to get to work.

Cora joins me at the front windows and we have the display set up in no time. I step back to admire our work and she bumps her shoulder against mine.

"We should go, or we'll be late," she points out, and I nod.

We both bundle up and wave goodbye to Saffron as we head out. It's a quiet, cold evening as we head down to the town square. The smell of pine and cinnamon hangs in the air, and a few snowflakes are starting to fall, lightly dusting the streets of Wolf Valley. It's the kind of picturesque setting that you'd find on the cover of a Christmas card, and under normal circumstances, I'd be soaking it all in.

But tonight, my mind is elsewhere.

"Where do you want us?" Cora calls to the organizer.

"Start on the lights, please!" She calls back, and we nod and get to work.

As we start stringing up lights and hanging garlands, I catch myself glancing around, half-expecting to see Kip lurking nearby. He's always been good at blending in, disappearing into the background, but now I wonder if I've been blind to his presence this whole time.

"It's really coming along, huh?" Cora asks, and I blink, looking around at the town square and all of our hard work.

"Yeah, it's nice."

"Hey," Cora says, nudging me with her elbow. "You okay? You've been quiet since we left the bookstore."

I shrug, trying to play it off. "Just thinking."

"About Kip?" she asks, her tone teasing but not unkind.

I sigh, shaking my head. "About the letters. About everything. What if... what if I'm wrong, Cora? What if it's not him? I don't want to make a fool of myself."

Cora's expression softens, and she tugs me over to the side, away from the others. "Ginger, you're not going to make a fool of yourself. Whoever this guy is, he clearly cares about you. He's been writing you letters for months. And if it is Kip... well, you'd be lucky to have him. He seems like a good guy."

I bite my lip, feeling the weight of her words. "I know he is. I just... I don't know if I'm ready."

Cora gives me a small, understanding smile. "You don't have to be ready right this second. But don't close yourself off, okay? You deserve to be happy, Ginger."

I nod, though my heart is still heavy with uncertainty. Cora's right, of course. Whoever this mystery man is, he's taken the time to get to know me, to write to me, to admire me from a distance. Maybe it's time I let myself open up to the possibility that someone—whether it's Kip or not—actually wants me.

By the time we finish decorating the square, I'm exhausted. I touch the most recent letter in my coat pocket, the paper crinkling against the fabric as I head toward my car. My sisters are meeting me later tonight for dinner, but for now, I just need a moment to clear my head.

The streets are quiet as I drive through town, my thoughts swirling like the snowflakes outside. When I finally pull into the driveway of Olive's house, I take a deep breath, steeling myself for the evening ahead.

I'm not sure what tomorrow will bring, or if I'll ever find out who's been writing me these letters. But there's one thing I do know.

I'm falling for him.

And if it's Kip... well, maybe that wouldn't be so bad after all.

THREE

Kip

I STAND IN THE SHADOWS, clutching the letter in my hand as if it's the only thing tethering me to reality. It's late, and the streets are empty, but my heart is pounding like I'm in the middle of a crowd, all eyes on me.

I shouldn't be here. I shouldn't be doing this. It's too risky. I know that she'll be out here any minute.

And yet, I have to.

I glance around, checking to make sure no one is watching, before I walk over to Ginger's car and slip the letter under her windshield wiper. My hands shake as I pull away, and for a second, I think about leaving. Not just this spot, but the whole thing—the letters, the secrets, the cowardice. But then Ginger's face flashes in my mind, the way her smile lights up everything around her. The way her eyes spark when she reads one of my notes, and I know I can't stop. Not now. It's a stupid, childish thing, leaving these letters for her, but it's all I have. It's the only way I can be close to her without actually having to face her.

I'm about to slip away when a sound startles me—a door slamming at the coffeehouse down the block. My heart jumps into my throat as I duck behind a nearby building, peeking around the corner just in time to see Ginger walking toward her car.

Shit. That was too close.

I press my back against the cold brick wall, holding my breath as she approaches her car. My pulse races as I watch her reach for the note I left behind. She pauses, her eyes scanning the parking lot for a second before she pulls the paper from under the wiper.

Something's wrong.

She's off today.

I watch her read the note, and my body starts to grow cold as I catalog her reaction.

She doesn't smile this time.

I frown, watching as she reads the letter, her brow furrowing. There's frustration in the way her shoulders tense, and I can feel the anxiety bubbling up inside me. She's been reading my letters for months now, but I've never seen her look like this.

She's upset.

I hate that I can't do anything about it. I hate that I'm too much of a coward to walk up to her, to tell her that it's me, that I'm the guy who's been pining for her from afar. Instead, I stand here, frozen in place, watching her.

I watch as she reads my note and takes a deep breath. She's not smiling like she usually is after I leave her and note, and a pit starts to form in my stomach, growing by the second as I watch her. She looks like she's debating something, and my mind races as I try to figure out what she's thinking.

Suddenly, Ginger pulls something out of her bag—a pen and a scrap of paper. My heart lurches as I watch her scribble something down, her movements quick and sharp, as if she's trying to get the words out before she changes her mind. Then, with a determined look, she tucks the note under her own windshield wiper and walks away.

I don't move. I don't breathe. I wait until she's disappeared down the street, my mind racing with what she could've written. Did she figure it out? Does she know it's me?

Or worse—does she want it to stop?

When she's long gone, I force myself to move, my legs stiff and heavy as I approach her car. My fingers tremble as I reach for the note she left behind, my pulse pounding in my ears. The moment I open it, my breath catches in my throat.

MEET ME.

THE WORDS ARE bold and underlined, like she's daring me to step out of the shadows. Like she's tired of waiting, tired of the mystery. She wants to know who I am, and now I'm faced with a choice I've been both dreading and looking forward to from the moment that I wrote that first letter.

I should be happy, right? I mean, if she wants to meet, then she must have liked my letters. She must be interested in me.

Right?

I've spent months dreaming about this moment, imagining what it would be like for her to finally know. But now that it's here, all I can feel is panic. My scars feel like they're burning under my skin, a constant reminder.

She thinks she's falling for someone who doesn't exist. The man in those letters isn't real. He's a fantasy, a version of myself that I'll never be. And if she finds out the truth... she'll hate me. She'll look at me like everyone else in town does—with pity, or worse, disgust.

I crumple the note in my hand, my chest tight with fear. Then I hurry to straighten it back out. I can't bear to destroy anything that Ginger gives to me.

What the hell am I supposed to do now? Do I meet her and risk everything? Or do I keep hiding, keep pretending that this is enough?

I know the answer. I've known it for a while now.

I can't keep hiding.

But the fear is paralyzing, and I'm not ready. Not yet.

With a heavy sigh, I shove the note into my pocket and head to my truck. I need to head to work and wrap up a few things, but even as I drive toward the helicopter hangar, my mind keeps drifting back to that note and the decision I'll have to make.

By the time I get to work, Huxley is already there, prepping one of the choppers for the morning flight. He glances up as I approach, wiping grease off his hands with a rag.

"Hey, wasn't expecting to see you here," he says with a grin. "Miss me?"

I grunt in response, trying to shake the tension from my shoulders as I grab my gear. I can feel his eyes on me, but I'm not in the mood to explain. Not yet.

"Everything okay?" Huxley asks, his voice softening. He knows me well enough to pick up on my mood, even when I try to hide it.

"Yeah," I mutter. "Just... stuff on my mind."

Huxley arches an eyebrow, but he doesn't push. Instead, he changes the subject, knowing that I'll talk when I'm ready.

"So, have you made a decision? Are you going to the town's holiday festival?" he asks, his tone casual. "The one with all the mistletoe and terrible music?" He asks as if I need a reminder.

I shrug, trying to play it off. "Maybe. I haven't decided yet. What about you?"

He snorts. "Hell no."

I glance over at him, narrowing my eyes. "Why not? No holiday spirit?"

"Not interested."

"Cora will be there," I point out, and he tenses.

We haven't talked about it much, but I've seen the way that he looks at her, and I know that he likes her just as much as I like Ginger.

"Did you get Ginger's car fixed last night?" He asks, and I nod. "How long did it take you?"

"Four hours, and you're changing the subject."

He sighs, tossing the rag onto a nearby table. "Fine, I'll go, and we both know that you're going. You'll show up, even if you keep your distance. Just like always."

I huff out a laugh, but it's forced. Huxley knows me too well. He knows I can't stay away from Ginger, even if it means lingering in the background, just out of sight. The idea of watching her laugh and smile with other people, of seeing her with someone else under the mistletoe—it makes my stomach twist.

But showing up? Actually talking to her, revealing that I'm the one behind the letters? I don't know if I have it in me.

"Yeah, maybe," I say, turning away from him and

focusing on the helicopter in front of me. "I'll think about it."

Huxley doesn't say anything, but I can feel his eyes on me, like he's waiting for me to make a decision. And maybe I am too.

As the night drags on, my mind keeps wandering back to that damn note in my pocket. The weight of it feels heavier with every passing hour. Ginger wants to meet, and if I don't show up, if I keep hiding, I'll lose her before I ever really had her.

But if I do show up... what then? What if she sees me and regrets everything? What if she realizes that the guy in the letters isn't the guy standing in front of her? Can I handle that rejection?

The doubt gnaws at me, refusing to let go.

By the time I finish up and head home, I'm no closer to an answer. I drive home in silence, the streets dark and empty, and all I can think about is the holiday party. I know Ginger will be there. I know she'll be waiting for me.

And I know I'm running out of time to decide what to do.

As I pull into my driveway, I lean my head back against the seat, closing my eyes for a moment. The house is quiet, empty, and for the first time in a long time, I feel the weight of my loneliness. I've spent so long pushing people away, hiding behind these letters, that I've forgotten what it's like to really be close to someone.

Ginger could change that. She could be the one to pull me out of this darkness.

If I'm brave enough to let her.

I glance at the note in my pocket one last time before heading inside. I'll have to make a choice soon.

But not tonight.

FOUR

Ginger

IT'S BEEN three days since I left my secret admirer the note, and still nothing.

I keep checking my car, mailbox, under my welcome mat and everywhere else that I can think about. I know that I'm driving my sisters crazy by looking all over their businesses every morning, every afternoon, even late at night after work, hoping—no, *praying*—that there will be something waiting for me. Another letter. A sign. *Anything*. But there's been nothing.

The note I left is gone, so I know he got it. He must've read it. He had to have seen that I asked to meet, and still nothing.

The silence has been deafening.

I don't know what I expected. Maybe I thought he'd be excited, that he'd jump at the chance to finally come out of the shadows and show me who he is, but that doesn't really make sense with the whole anonymous letter thing that he's been doing. I guess I had just hoped that he would want to meet face-to-face, to talk about all of this.

Instead, all I'm left with is doubt and frustration, wondering if I crossed some invisible line. Did I scare him off? Was it too much too soon? Or maybe he's not the person I imagined him to be. Maybe he doesn't want to meet at all.

That thought makes my chest tighten, and I hate it. I hate how much I've let myself get attached to a man I've never even met, how much I've invested in the words of a stranger. But I can't help it. Every letter he's written feels like a piece of him, and I've been falling in love with those pieces for months now.

I can't just let it go. Not yet.

With a determined breath, I grab a pen and a sheet of paper from behind the counter of Wet and Wild, my sister Maple's adult toy store. I was here covering for her while she went out to lunch with her boyfriend, Ryder. She just got back, though, so I know that I'll be headed out soon. Maple is in the back, working on some inventory, and I'm thankful for the moment of privacy. I scribble down the words quickly, not letting myself overthink it.

MEET ME. **I'm not waiting any longer. I need to know who you are.**

I STARE at the note for a long moment, my fingers tightening around the edges of the paper. This is it—my last attempt, my last push. If he doesn't reply after this, I'll have to let it go. I'll have to accept that maybe I'm just chasing a fantasy, a ghost.

But I need to try.

I fold the note carefully, slipping it into my bag. I'll leave it on my car after work, just like I did the last time, and hope that this time, he'll be brave enough to answer.

When I head into the back room, Maple looks up from her computer, raising an eyebrow as I approach.

"You okay? You've been kind of... off today."

I force a smile, though it feels weak, like I can't quite muster the energy to fake it. "Yeah, I'm fine. Just... thinking about stuff."

She narrows her eyes, clearly not buying it. "Is this about your secret admirer again?"

I sigh, leaning against the counter as I cross my arms. "Yeah. I left him a note a few days ago, asking him to meet me, but I haven't heard anything. I'm starting to think I messed up."

Maple frowns, setting aside the stack of lingerie she was organizing. "Why would you think that? Maybe he's just nervous."

"Or maybe he doesn't want to meet me," I say, the bitterness creeping into my voice. "Maybe he's been having fun with the mystery and doesn't actually want anything more."

My sister gives me a sympathetic look, but before she can say anything, the bell over the door jingles, and Cora walks in, her face lighting up when she spots me.

"Ginger! I've been looking for you all afternoon," she says, bounding over to the counter with a grin. "Got time for a coffee break?"

I glance over at Maple, who waves me off with a smile. "Go ahead. I've got it covered from here. Thanks for helping out today."

"Anytime."

With a sigh of relief, I grab my coat and bag, following Cora out of the sex shop. The crisp winter air bites at my cheeks, and for a moment, the cold wakes me up, shaking off some of the frustration I've been carrying around all day.

Cora nudges me as we walk. "So, what's the latest with your mystery man?"

I groan, pulling the folded note from my bag and waving it in front of her. "Still nothing. I'm leaving him another note today, basically demanding that he meet me in person. I'm tired of waiting."

Cora's eyes widen in surprise, and then she grins. "Good for you! It's about time you took charge."

"Yeah, well, if this doesn't work, I don't know what will. I've been falling for this guy, Cora, and I don't even know who he is. It's ridiculous."

She gives me a sympathetic look as we walk into the coffee shop, the smell of roasted beans and cinnamon immediately wrapping around us. We order our usual drinks and settle into a booth by the window, the snow lightly falling outside as people bustle around the square, decorating for the holiday festival.

"Have you thought about, you know, putting yourself out there?" Cora asks, her tone gentle but probing.

"What do you mean?" I ask, sipping my coffee.

"I mean, maybe it's time to meet someone, Ginger. In person. Secret admirers are fun and romantic, but they're not exactly... real. You don't even know if this guy is who you think he is."

I frown, swirling my coffee in its cup. "You think I should just... move on? Start dating other people?"

Cora shrugs. "Maybe. Look, you've been waiting for months, and you're still waiting. What if he never shows up? You deserve to be happy, and you deserve someone who's willing to put themselves out there for you."

I know she's right. As much as I want to believe that my mystery man will come forward, there's no guarantee. And I can't keep putting my life on hold for someone who might never appear.

"I don't know," I say, leaning back in my seat. "It feels weird, starting over, dating someone new when I'm still hung up on this."

Cora grins, her eyes twinkling with mischief. "You know what you need? A little liquid courage."

I laugh, shaking my head. "Oh no. I know where this is going."

But Cora is already up, pulling me out of the booth. "Come on. We're going to your place, and we're going to have some fun. You need to loosen up a bit, Ginger. Trust me."

I groan, but I don't resist. Maybe she's right. Maybe a night of letting loose is exactly what I need to get out of my own head.

Two hours and a bottle of wine later, Cora and I are sprawled out on my couch, giggling like schoolgirls as we scroll through dating profiles on my laptop.

"I can't believe we're doing this," I say, covering my face with my hands as Cora types furiously on the keyboard.

"You need to put yourself out there," she says, laughing as she adds another detail to my profile. That's been her mantra tonight. I swear that she's told me the same thing a dozen times in the last two hours, and she just keeps repeating it as she gets even more drunk.

I groan, but I can't help but laugh along with her. I'm definitely tipsy, my head buzzing pleasantly from the wine, and for the first time in days, I'm not thinking about my mystery man. I'm not obsessing over the letters or the lack of a response. Instead, I'm just... here, in the moment, laughing with my best friend.

"Okay, let's see," Cora says, reading off the screen. "Loves Christmas, works at a bookstore, a bakery, and an adult toy store, terrible at dating—check, check, and check."

I snort, rolling my eyes. "Thanks for that glowing endorsement. I'll have guys hitting me up left and right with that bio!"

Cora grins, setting the laptop down on the coffee table. "It will work and you'll thank me later. Besides, if this doesn't work out, we'll just delete it. No harm, no foul."

I sigh, leaning back against the cushions, feeling a little lighter than I have in days. "I guess you're right. Maybe this is what I need."

"Exactly," Cora says, her voice slurring slightly as she grabs her glass. "Now, let's just relax and let the magic happen."

I smile, closing my eyes as the warmth of the wine settles over me, making my limbs heavy and my mind foggy. Cora leans her head on my shoulder, and before I know it, the sounds of the world start to fade away, and I'm drifting off to sleep.

When I wake up the next morning, my head throbs, and the first thing I see is Cora sprawled out on the floor, snoring softly. The empty bottle of wine sits on the coffee table, and my laptop is still open to my brand-new dating profile.

I groan, rubbing my temples as I sit up, the events of last night slowly coming back to me. I glance at the clock and realize I'm late to help Olive out at the bakery—really late.

Shit.

I scramble off the couch, nudging Cora with my foot as I try to gather my bearings. "Cora, wake up. We overslept."

She groans, burying her face in the couch cushions. "Five more minutes..."

I laugh despite the pounding in my head, and as I rush to get ready for the day, I can't help but feel nervous. I'm not ready to try online dating, not when I'm still so hung up on my secret admirer.

What other choice do I have, though? If he won't meet me, then I need to try something else. Who knows, maybe putting myself out there won't be such a bad idea after all.

FIVE

Kip

I THOUGHT I had more time. I thought I could delay meeting her a little longer, could maybe come up with the perfect way to reveal myself.

But then I found out about the dating profile.

When Huxley told me, I almost didn't believe him. He'd mentioned it in passing, as if it were no big deal, but my heart had dropped like a stone. Ginger Baker, my Ginger, had made an online dating profile. And now, the thought of her meeting some random guy, letting him get close to her—*my* girl—it was driving me insane.

I shouldn't be this angry. I know that. But I can't help it. After all these months of writing to her, pouring out everything I'm too afraid to say in person, the thought of someone else stepping in where I haven't had the courage to go... it's too much.

I grab my phone, my hands shaking with frustration as I open the dating app Huxley mentioned. It takes me a few minutes to find her, but when I do, my stomach twists. There she is, smiling at the camera, her profile casual and sweet, just like her.

I stare at the screen, my heart pounding as I hover over the message button. This is a terrible idea. I shouldn't be doing this. But I can't stop myself. My thumb taps the button, and before I know it, I'm typing out the first thing that comes to mind.

TAKE YOUR DATING PROFILE DOWN.

I HIT SEND BEFORE I can think better of it, my pulse racing as I wait for her to respond. What the hell am I doing? This isn't the way to handle this, but I can't shake the fear gnawing at me—the fear of losing her before I've even had a chance to show her who I really am.

The phone buzzes in my hand, and I look down at her reply.

EXCUSE ME? *Why? Who is this?*

I SWALLOW HARD, my mind racing as I try to figure out what to say next. I can't exactly tell her the truth, not yet. But I also can't stand the idea of her going out with someone else. I clench my jaw and type out my next message.

THE GUY *who's been writing to you. Take the profile down.*

. . .

THERE'S A LONG PAUSE, and I wonder if I've crossed a line. My palms are sweating, and I almost want to take it all back, but then her reply comes through, and I can practically feel the heat in her words.

YOU'RE *the one who's been leaving me notes, and now you think you can just tell me what to do? Who do you think you are?*

I GROAN, running a hand through my hair. This is going terribly. I take a deep breath and type out my reply, trying to explain myself without sounding like a complete asshole.

I DON'T WANT *you to meet anyone else. I'll explain everything, just… take the profile down.*

THERE'S ANOTHER LONG PAUSE, and I can almost hear the frustration in her silence. When her next message comes through, it's clear she's had enough.

EITHER YOU MEET *me under the mistletoe at the town holiday party at 9 PM, or I'm done taking orders from you. If you don't show, I'm putting this profile to good use.*

. . .

MY HEART LURCHES in my chest as I read her words, the ultimatum hanging in the air like a threat. She's not playing around anymore. I've pushed her too far, and now I'm backed into a corner. I either meet her at the party, face-to-face, or I lose her.

I close my eyes, my chest tight with anxiety. This is it. I've run out of time.

I stare at the screen, my fingers hovering over the keyboard. There's so much I want to say, but none of it feels right. In the end, I don't reply. I can't. I have to figure this out, and the clock is ticking.

I'm so worked up, and I know that I need to find something to keep busy, so I head to work. I find Huxley in the garage, tinkering with one of the helicopters. He glances up as I approach, wiping grease off his hands with a rag.

"Hey, you look like you've seen a ghost. What's up?"

I pace back and forth, the anxiety gnawing at me. "I messed up, man. She's going to be at the holiday party. She told me I either meet her there at 9 PM, or she's done."

Huxley raises an eyebrow, leaning against the work-bench. "And you're freaking out because...?"

I glare at him. "Because I'm not ready, Hux. I can't just show up and... what if she takes one look at me and regrets everything? What if I ruin this? I mean, she's expecting some handsome, charming guy and I'm--," I throw my hands out, my words cutting off.

He lets out a sigh, crossing his arms over his chest. "Kip, you've been writing to her for months. She's falling for you, not some other guy. If she's into you in those letters, she's going to be into you in person. You're over-thinking this."

I shake my head, the doubts swirling in my mind. "You don't know that. The guy she's falling for isn't the real me.

It's the version of me that I wish I could be, the guy who isn't broken."

Huxley rolls his eyes. "You're not broken, Kip. And she'll see that. You just have to show up."

I stop pacing, staring down at the floor. "What if I don't go?"

Huxley's expression hardens. "Then you lose her. And you'll spend the rest of your life wondering what could've happened if you'd just had the guts to show up."

I swallow hard, the weight of his words sinking in. He's right. If I don't go, if I let my fear win, I'll lose Ginger forever. And I can't let that happen.

"I have to go, don't I?" I say, my voice barely above a whisper.

Huxley grins. "Yep. And it's going to be fine. Hell, this could be the best Christmas of your life."

"Or the worst," I mutter, rubbing the back of my neck. The thought of standing under the mistletoe, waiting for Ginger to show up, only for her to take one look at me and walk away—it's terrifying.

Huxley slaps me on the back. "Come on, man. You've got this. And hey, maybe we can make it easier on you. You know, blend in a little."

I frown, not understanding what he's getting at. "What do you mean?"

Huxley's grin widens. "We'll volunteer to help out with the party. That way, you can be there without all the pressure of just waiting around. You'll have something to do, and you'll look like a hero for helping out. Win-win."

I blink at him, considering the idea. It's not a terrible plan. Volunteering would give me an excuse to be there, to keep myself busy, and maybe it would help with the nerves. And if it means I get to be closer to Ginger, even better.

"Yeah, okay," I say slowly, nodding. "I'll do it. But... I'm not sure this is going to end well."

Huxley laughs, slinging an arm around my shoulders as we head out of the garage. "Hey, worst case, you get rejected, and we go to your place and get drunk. Best case, you get the girl. Either way, you'll finally know, and you can stop living in limbo."

I shake my head, but I can't help the small smile tugging at my lips. He's right. This is it—the moment I've been avoiding for months. It's either going to be the best Christmas I've ever had, or the worst.

I just have to show up.

SIX

Ginger

I STRETCH ON MY TOES, trying to hang the last string of lights along the rafters, but of course, the bulbs decide to burn out right as I'm almost done. I groan in frustration, letting the string drop from my hands and dangle uselessly. There's always something, isn't there?

It's just a few days before the big holiday party, and the town square is buzzing with last-minute preparations. I've been volunteering for hours, trying to make sure everything is perfect for the event. The twinkling lights, the pine-scented garlands, the mistletoe—it's supposed to feel magical, but right now, all I feel is exhausted.

I grab the burned-out string of lights and start untangling them, but my thoughts are far from the task at hand. The note I left for my secret admirer is still on my mind. It's been days since I demanded that he meet me under the mistletoe at the party, and I haven't heard a word back. I know he took my last note, but the silence since then has been eating away at me.

What if he doesn't show up? What if he just... disappears?

"Uh...need a hand with that?"

The deep voice jolts me out of my thoughts, and I look up, startled. Standing just a few feet away are Kip and Huxley, both of them dressed casually but looking like they belong in a magazine spread for rugged, outdoorsy men. I wasn't expecting them, and the sight of Kip—his broad shoulders, his quiet confidence—sends a shiver down my spine.

"Oh, uh, yeah," I stammer, holding up the string of lights. "These decided to burn out on me."

Kip steps forward, his expression calm but focused as he takes the lights from my hands. He angles his head to the right, and I know that he's trying to hide the scars that mar that side of his face and neck. It's obvious that he's self-conscious about them, but I don't know why. It makes him look edgy and sexy.

His fingers brush mine for a split second, and I feel a spark of warmth shoot through me. "I'll take care of it," he says, his voice low and rough.

I glance at Cora, who's been helping me decorate, and she gives me a wide-eyed look before quickly turning her attention back to a garland she's hanging on the light post outside of the Nosh Diner. I can tell she's trying not to smirk.

Kip carefully inspects the lights, his brow furrowed in concentration as he works on replacing the burned-out bulbs. Huxley, meanwhile, is chatting with some of the other volunteers, making jokes and keeping things light as usual. But my attention is locked on Kip.

"Should be good now," he says, pulling me out of my thoughts. He plugs in the lights, and they flicker to life, casting a soft, warm glow over the room.

"Thanks," I say, smiling up at him. "You're a lifesaver."

He shrugs, offering me a small smile in return. "No problem."

For a moment, we just stand there, the twinkling lights between us, and I can't help but feel a strange sense of connection. It's quiet, but it's there—a warmth, an understanding. I wonder if he feels it too, or if it's just my imagination running wild.

"So, are you helping out with the festival?" I ask, trying to keep the conversation going.

Kip nods, glancing around at the decorations. "Yeah. Huxley and I thought we'd lend a hand."

"Well, it's good to have more volunteers," I say, hoping I don't sound as nervous as I feel. "This place is going to look amazing once we're done."

He nods again, his eyes scanning the block, but there's something thoughtful in his gaze, like he's thinking about something else entirely. I want to ask him what's on his mind, but I don't. Instead, I focus on the task at hand, hanging more lights and garlands while we work side by side in comfortable silence.

At one point, our hands brush again as we both reach for the same string of lights, and I feel my heart skip a beat. I glance up at him, and for a split second, I think I see something flicker in his eyes—something more than just casual friendliness.

Could he feel the same way about me? Could he...?

No, stop it, Ginger. Don't let your mind go there. He's probably just being nice.

But the thought lingers, and as we finish hanging the

last of the decorations, I find myself wishing—*hoping*—that Kip could be the one behind the letters. It would make sense, wouldn't it? He's always around, always so quiet and careful. And the way he looks at me sometimes...

"Ready to head out?" Kip's voice breaks through my thoughts, and I blink, realizing that we've finished. The town square looks magical now, the lights twinkling and the decorations perfectly in place.

I glance at Cora, who's already putting on her coat. "Yeah, I'm ready."

Kip walks with me as we step out into the cold night, our breaths visible in the frosty air. The snow has started falling again, soft and gentle, blanketing the streets in white. It's beautiful, the kind of night that makes you want to hold someone close and never let go.

We walk in silence for a while, our footsteps crunching in the snow. I sneak glances at Kip, wondering if he's going to say something, if he feels the same pull I do. There's a tension between us—something unspoken but undeniable.

When we reach my front door, I stop, turning to face him. My heart is pounding, and I'm not sure why I'm so nervous. He looks down at me, his eyes unreadable in the dim light, and for a moment, I think he might kiss me.

I *want* him to kiss me.

But he doesn't. He hesitates, then gives me a small, almost shy smile. "Goodnight, Ginger."

Disappointment floods me, but I force a smile. "Goodnight, Kip."

He lingers for a second longer, as if he's debating something, but then he turns and walks away, his figure disappearing into the falling snow.

I watch him go, my heart aching in my chest. Part of me wonders if I should have said something, done something to close the distance between us. But instead, I turn the key in my door and step inside, the warmth of the house doing nothing to ease the chill in my chest.

I lean against the door, closing my eyes as I replay the night in my mind. I don't know if Kip will ever see me the way I see him, or if my secret admirer will ever reveal himself.

But for now, I'll keep hoping. Maybe, just maybe, this Christmas will bring me the love I've been waiting for.

And if Kip *is* my secret admirer... well, that would be the best gift of all.

SEVEN

Kip

I ALMOST KISSED her last night.

It was so close, I could feel the electricity in the air between us. Her eyes were soft, full of hope and warmth, and I swear my heart stopped when she looked up at me like that. But I chickened out. My feet moved before my brain could catch up, and I walked away like an idiot.

Now, it's two days until the holiday party, and I can't stop thinking about it. About her. About kissing her and doing a hell of a lot more than that to her.

I'm back at the town hall, helping Huxley and the girls finish up the last of the decorations. The square is coming together beautifully, with garlands, lights, and other decorations strung along the lamp posts and buildings, and the smell of pine and cinnamon filling the air. But I can't focus on any of it. All I can think about is how close I was to kissing Ginger, how her lips would have felt against mine, how she might have—

"Yo, Kip, you spacing out?" Huxley's voice cuts through my thoughts, and I shake my head, trying to snap back to the present.

"Nah, just... focusing," I mutter, grabbing another string of lights and draping them over a nearby archway.

"Thinking about Ginger?" Huxley asks with a knowing smirk.

I grunt in response, which only makes him chuckle.

As we work, I catch glimpses of Ginger across the square. She's helping with the mistletoe, her auburn hair catching the light as she laughs with Cora. Every time she smiles, it feels like a punch to my chest. She's beautiful, in that effortless way that makes it hard to look at her without wanting more.

And then, just as I'm starting to focus again, I see them—two guys, strangers, walking up to her. They're laughing, chatting her up, their eyes lingering on her in a way that makes my blood boil.

I set down the lights, my jaw clenching as I watch them. One of the guys steps closer to Ginger, and I can see the way her smile falters, her discomfort clear.

That's it.

Before I even realize what I'm doing, I'm moving toward them, my fists clenched at my sides. When I reach them, I step right between Ginger and the guys, my eyes cold as I look at them.

"You need something?" I ask, my voice low and dangerous.

The guys glance at each other, clearly not expecting to be interrupted. "Uh, we were just—"

"You were just leaving," I growl, cutting them off.

They stare at me for a moment, but one look at my face is enough to make them reconsider. With mumbled excuses, they back off and shuffle away, leaving me standing there, fuming.

"Wow," Ginger says from behind me, her voice soft with surprise. "That was... intense."

I turn to face her, my anger fading the moment I see her face. She's not upset—if anything, she looks amused. "Sorry," I mutter, running a hand through my hair. "They were bothering you."

She smiles, a real one this time, and it sends a wave of warmth through me. "Thanks, Kip. But I could've handled it."

"I know," I say, trying not to sound too defensive. "But I didn't like the way they were looking at you."

Her smile softens, and for a moment, we just stand there, the noise of the town fading into the background. There's something between us, something I can't quite put into words, but it's there. It's always been there.

"Hey, I need to head back to the bookstore for a bit," Ginger says, breaking the silence. "Want to walk with me?"

I nod, eager for any excuse to spend more time with her. "Sure."

We leave the town hall together, the cold winter air biting at our faces as we walk down the snow-covered streets. It's quiet, the town peaceful in the early evening, and for once, I feel calm. Just being near her makes everything feel right.

As we reach the bookstore, something catches my eye—mistletoe, hanging just above the door. My heart skips a beat, and I glance at Ginger, wondering if she's noticed it too.

She does. Her eyes flick up to the mistletoe, then back to me, a nervous smile playing on her lips.

This is it. No backing out this time.

I take a step closer to her, my heart pounding in my chest as I reach for her hand. She doesn't pull away. If anything, she steps closer too, her breath visible in the cold air between us.

And then, without overthinking it, I lean in and press my lips to hers.

It's soft at first, tentative, like we're both testing the waters. But then she kisses me back, and everything else disappears. The cold, the snow, the world—it's all gone, replaced by the warmth of her lips, the way she fits perfectly against me.

It feels right. More right than anything has in a long time.

When we finally pull apart, my heart is racing, and I can see the same surprise in her eyes that I feel. For a moment, I wonder if she knows—if she realizes that I'm the one who's been writing to her all these months.

But before I can say anything, she smiles, and it's like the whole world lights up. "I guess that's what happens under mistletoe, huh?"

I chuckle, though my mind is still racing. "Yeah, I guess so."

We stand there for a moment longer, the weight of the kiss lingering between us, but then she steps back, her smile soft and shy. "I should get back to work."

"Right," I say, nodding. "I'll, uh... see you later?"

She nods, her cheeks flushed as she heads into the bookstore. I stand there for a second, watching her disappear behind the door, and I can't help but wonder—did she kiss me because she wanted to? Or was it just because of the mistletoe?

The question gnaws at me as I turn and walk away, my mind spinning with uncertainty. Does she like me? Or is she just caught up in the tradition, the magic of the season?

I head towards work, the snow crunching beneath my boots as I try to make sense of it all. By the time I reach the garage, Huxley is there, working on one of the helicopters.

"How'd it go with Ginger?" he asks, not looking up from the engine.

I hesitate, the memory of the kiss still fresh in my mind. "We kissed."

Huxley looks up, eyebrows raised. "Seriously? That's great, man!"

I shrug, though my heart is still pounding. "Yeah, but... I don't know. It was under mistletoe. What if it was just because of that? What if she doesn't actually..."

Huxley shakes his head, grinning. "Come on, Kip. If she kissed you, it's not just because of mistletoe. Trust me."

I don't respond, the doubts still lingering in the back of my mind. But then Huxley changes the subject, his grin widening.

"Speaking of girls, I need your help with something."

I raise an eyebrow. "With what?"

He rubs the back of his neck, looking unusually sheepish. "Cora."

I laugh, shaking my head. "You're finally admitting it, huh?"

"Yeah, yeah," Huxley mutters, though there's a smile on his face. "But I have no idea what to do. She's... difficult."

I snort. "Difficult? She's perfect for you, and you know it."

"Maybe, but she's also impossible to figure out. Every time I try to get close, she pushes me away. What am I supposed to do?"

I think for a moment, then grin. "Stop pissing her off, for one."

Huxley laughs, shaking his head. "Yeah, well, easier said than done."

We spend the next hour brainstorming ideas, throwing out everything from grand romantic gestures to simple conversations. But in the back of my mind, all I can think about is Ginger. That kiss. And whether or not she feels the same way I do.

Because in two days, I'll know for sure.

The holiday party is coming up, and everything will be decided under that mistletoe.

Best or worst Christmas ever—I guess I'm about to find out.

EIGHT

Ginger

IT'S the day of the holiday party, and I can't stop thinking about the kiss.

For two days, that moment has been playing on a loop in my mind. The warmth of his lips, the way he stepped close to me under the mistletoe, how my heart raced like it was about to burst out of my chest. I've been floating on this strange, giddy feeling ever since, and no matter how much I try to focus on anything else, all I can think about is *Kip*.

And his kiss.

And the fact that he's my secret admirer. He's the man who wrote me such sweet words, who made me feel special and seen and beautiful. I know it.

I've been helping set up for the party all day, but my mind keeps drifting. Every time I pass the mistletoe, my stomach flips, because tonight... tonight is the night.

Will he show? Will he admit that he's the one who has been sending me letters?

It's almost 9 PM, and the party is in full swing, with people milling about, grabbing hot chocolate and other treats, and looking at the little vendor tables. But I'm standing here, waiting. Waiting for Kip to show up, waiting for him to kiss me again.

I already know it's him. I knew the moment I saw how he reacted to those guys flirting with me. The jealousy in his eyes, the way he stepped in without hesitation—that's when it clicked. The guy I'd been hoping for, the guy I'd been falling in love with through words, was Kip all along.

Now, I just need him to show up.

I glance around the town square, feeling that familiar twinge of nerves. The twinkling lights, the smell of cinnamon and pine, the sound of laughter and Christmas carols—it's all perfect. But my heart is pounding, and I can't focus on any of it. All I care about is *him*.

I check the clock again. Two minutes to nine. My hands are sweaty, and my heart is racing. I've never been this nervous in my life.

And then, I see him.

Kip walks through the crowd, looking as nervous as I feel. His dark hair is a little messy from the cold wind, and his strong jaw is clenched like he's trying to steel himself for something. He's scanning the space, and when his eyes land on me, his whole body seems to relax, even if it's just for a moment.

He starts walking toward me, but before he can get too far, I do the only thing I can think of—I run.

I don't wait for him to reach the mistletoe. I don't care about anything else in this moment. All I care about is *him*. I run across the square, my boots slipping slightly on the icy sidewalk, and when I reach him, I leap into his arms.

He catches me, his eyes wide with surprise, but I don't

give him time to react. I press my lips to his, and everything else falls away. The music, the people, the noise—it's all gone, replaced by the warmth of his kiss.

His arms tighten around me, holding me close, and I can feel his heart pounding in his chest. When we finally pull apart, I'm breathless, and I can see the shock in his eyes.

"I love your letters," I whisper, my hands still resting on his shoulders.

He blinks, looking like I've just knocked the wind out of him. "You... you knew?"

I smile, my heart swelling with affection for him. "I figured it out the other day when you got all jealous about those guys talking to me. Plus, when I showed Saffron the stationery, she told me that you were the only one to buy it in the last few months."

His brow furrows. "They were hitting on you."

I roll my eyes, laughing softly. "They were just talking to me. You didn't need to scare them off."

He shakes his head, a small grin tugging at his lips. "Trust me, they weren't just talking."

I tighten my hold on him, and uncertainty flashes across his face.

"Are you disappointed?" He whispers, and I bite my lip, feeling the butterflies in my stomach fluttering wildly.

"Well... I was kind of hoping it was you."

His eyes widen.

"Really?"

"Yeah, why are you so surprised?"

His finger absently runs across the scars on his face, and my heart hurts.

"I don't mind your scars. I like them. They make you look like a badass. Plus, it means that you can scare off any guys who try to flirt with me."

"Damn right," he growls, and I giggle.

He smiles at me softly, his whole face softening, and I can see it then. He loves me. He would do anything for me.

"I'll always protect you, Ginger."

"I know," I whisper, and for a moment, we just stand there, staring at each other.

The space feels small, like it's just the two of us, and I can't help but feel like everything has been leading to this moment.

"I can't believe you figured it out," Kip says, his voice low and a little shy. "I thought I was doing a pretty good job of hiding it."

I laugh, shaking my head. "You were... until you weren't."

"Yeah, I was starting to crack. It was hard being close to you, but not close enough," he says with a chuckle, but then his expression shifts, turning more serious. "I wanted to tell you. I just... I didn't know if you'd want me."

I feel my heart ache at the vulnerability in his voice. How could he ever think I wouldn't want him? Kip has always been the one I wanted, even when I didn't know it was him behind the letters.

"I've always wanted you," I whisper, my voice trembling with emotion. "You don't have to hide from me, Kip. I like you... and your letters."

His eyes widen at my words, and before I can say anything else, he kisses me again, pulling me closer, his lips soft and warm against mine. It's perfect. It's everything I've been dreaming of.

But then a shiver runs down my spine, the cold seeping into my bones from standing still in the cold, away from the heaters and crowd. Kip pulls back, concern flickering in his eyes.

"You're cold," he says, his voice soft as he starts to shrug off his coat.

I laugh, shaking my head. "I have a better idea for how you could warm me up," I say suggestively.

His eyebrows lift in surprise, but then a slow, hopeful, smile spreads across his face. "Oh yeah?"

"Uh-huh," I nod, biting my lip as I take his hand and start leading him toward the parking lot. "Let me tell you about it on the way to your place."

The cold winter air hits us as we step away from the buildings, but it doesn't matter. I've never felt warmer in my life, because tonight, I'm with Kip.

We can't stop smiling at each other as we make the short drive to Kip's house. He lives on the outskirts of town, next to his business, Semper Fly.

"I should have taken my car so you don't have to drive me back to town," I say as we pull into his driveway.

"That old thing might have never made it all of the way out here," he grunts, and I laugh.

"It's actually been running pretty smoothly lately!" I tell him, and he shakes his head.

"No, it hasn't," he grumbles quietly and it clicks then.

"Oh. My. God," I gasp as I turn to face him. "You've been sneaking around and fixing my car!"

He blushes, actually blushes, and clears his throat.

"Yeah, I didn't want you driving around in an unreliable car."

"How many times?" I ask him, my mind racing as I try to remember all of the times when my car wouldn't start or when it seemed like it was starting to act up and then magically was fine.

"I don't know. A few."

"It had to be more than just a few! I mean..." I trail off as I count in my head. "Jeez, Kip, it had to have been like once a month for the last six months at least."

"It's not a big deal," he grumbles, and I shake my head.

"Yes. It is. That was so... amazing of you. You're so sweet, Kip. Thank you."

He nods, and we stare at each other in the dark cab of his truck. I'm not sure who moves first, but soon we're both leaning over the center console, our lips a breath apart.

"Ginger..." His voice is low and rough like he's holding back.

I don't wait. I can't.

Without thinking, I reach for him, my hand sliding up his neck as I lean over the console. I feel the warmth of his skin beneath my fingers, the roughness of his jawline, and before I know it, my lips are on his.

The moment our mouths meet, it's like everything else falls away. The world outside the truck disappears, leaving only the heat of his kiss, the way his lips move against mine with such intensity it makes my head spin. He kisses me back, his hand tangling in my hair as he pulls me closer, and it's like we're both caught in this moment—wild, breathless, unstoppable.

I don't think I've ever wanted someone like this, felt this kind of urgency. My heart is racing, my whole body trembling as I press against him, deepening the kiss. His lips are soft, warm, and when I feel his tongue brush against mine, a shiver runs down my spine. I can't get enough of him. I never want this to stop.

Kip groans softly against my mouth, and the sound sends a jolt of electricity through me. His other hand slides to my waist, gripping me firmly as he pulls me even closer, like he's afraid I'll slip away. But I'm not going anywhere. I want to be right here, in this moment, with him.

I shift in my seat, turning toward him, my hands roaming over his chest, feeling the solid muscle beneath his shirt. He's strong, every inch of him, and it drives me wild knowing he's holding back for me, controlling that strength even as the tension between us builds.

"Kip..." I whisper against his lips, my breath ragged, my heart pounding. His name comes out like a plea, and he responds by kissing me harder, deeper, his fingers tightening in my hair.

I don't know how long we kiss—seconds, minutes, it could be hours for all I know. Time doesn't seem to matter when I'm with him like this, lost in the feel of him, the taste of him. The windows of the truck fog up, the world outside blurring into nothingness as we lose ourselves in each other.

When we finally break apart, we're both breathless, our foreheads resting against each other as we struggle to catch our breath. My lips feel swollen, tingling from the heat of the kiss, and my heart is still racing in my chest.

Kip looks at me, his eyes dark with desire, his breath warm against my skin. "I've been wanting to do that all night," he murmurs, his voice rough with need.

I smile, my fingers still tracing the line of his jaw, my own desire mirrored in his gaze. "Me too."

For a moment, we just stay like that, our bodies pressed close, the heat between us still simmering. I can feel his heart pounding against mine, and there's a part of me that wants more. I decide to listen to that part of me.

"Let's go inside," I whisper, and he nods.

We climb out of the truck, and he rushes over to my side, helping me down and taking my hand as we head up to the front porch.

He unlocks the door and ushers me in ahead of him. I scan his place, as I take off my jacket, hat, and mittens, taking in the mostly bare living room and kitchen.

"Nice place."

"Thanks."

He turns on some lights, and I wander further into the house.

"Want the tour?" He asks, and I nod. "Well, you've already seen the living room and kitchen."

I nod. "Very nice."

He takes my hand, and we head down the long hallway.

"This is the guest bathroom," he says, nudging the first door open. "And this is the first guest bedroom...and the second," he says, pushing open the next two doors. "And this... is my room."

I step into his room, and the tension between us grows as I wander closer to the king-size bed. The bed is neatly made, the corners of the dark blue comforter perfectly folded down, and I wonder if that was a habit that he always had or if he picked it up in the military.

"I like it."

"You can change anything that you don't like about the house," he says instantly.

I laugh, thinking that he's joking, but I turn to see him watching me with a serious look on his face.

"Wait, what?"

"Ginger," he starts, his voice low and rough. "I need to tell you something."

I nod, starting to get nervous as he shifts. He looks so anxious and I wonder what it is that he has to tell me.

"I... I've been falling in love with you," he tells me, the words coming out in a rush, like they've been trapped inside him for too long. "For a long time now."

My eyes widen, but not in shock.

"I love you," he says, his voice barely above a whisper. "I just needed you to know."

"I do know," I tell him. "I know, and I love you too. So much."

"So much?" He asks quietly, and I nod.

"So much."

For a moment, there's silence. Then, without warning, he leans forward, his lips crashing against mine in a kiss that's filled with everything—every unspoken word, every emotion we've both been holding back all these months.

It's soft at first, tentative, like we're testing the waters, but then something shifts. His hands tangle in my hair, pulling me closer, and I feel the heat between us ignite like a spark catching flame. I kiss him back with everything I have, pouring months of longing into every movement, every touch.

My body presses against his, and I feel him groan against my lips, the sound sending a rush of heat through me. His hands slide down to my waist as we deepen the kiss, my heart pounding in my chest. He feels so good, so *right*.

We break apart for air, our breaths coming in ragged gasps, and when I look into his dark blue eyes, I see everything—desire, love, tenderness, all mixed together in a way that makes my heart swell.

"I love you, Kip," I whisper as his forehead rests against mine. "I think I've loved you from your first letter."

We kiss again, slower this time, more deliberate, like we're savoring the moment. My hands roam over his chest, and I feel his pulse quicken, the heat between us growing with every passing second. I wonder if he can feel me trembling slightly as my fingers tighten in his shirt.

The kiss deepens, passion flaring hot and fast between us, and I lose myself in him—his touch, his scent, the sounds he makes as he holds me close. Nothing else matters. It's just us here in this moment, and I never want it to end.

Kip's hands slide down to my hips and toy with the hem of my sweater. I hum against his lips in agreement and a moment later, he's slipping the soft wool sweater over my head and tossing it aside. We stare at each other, both of us breathing hard. The lust is palpable in the air around us, and I feel like I'm burning up alive as he stares at me.

"I want you so fucking bad, Ginger," he whispers, and I swallow hard and nod.

"I'm yours. Take me."

That's all it takes and it's like a flip switches in Kip. He takes charge. There are no more soft kisses; it's all passion. I can taste his desperate need for me on his lips, and it drives me wild.

"Naked," he grunts at me, and I nod, scrambling to push my plaid leggings down my legs and kick them off. My thick wool socks follow, and then my panties.

"Bra," he orders as he drops to his knees at the edge of the bed.

I arch, reaching to unhook my bra, and his big hands grip my thighs, yanking me to the edge of the mattress. I blink, my brain trying to keep up with everything that he's doing.

"Kip," I breathe a second before he leans forward and buries his face in my pussy. "Fuck!" I shout, my bra long forgotten.

He's so enthusiastic as he licks me, practically devours me, and all I can do is lay there and let him have his way with me. So many emotions and feelings are building inside of me as his tongue licks over my clit, sucking the little pearl into his mouth.

"Kip! Oh, God," I gasp, moaning his name as his fingers spread me wider.

"So damn sweet," he moans against my core, and I grip the bedspread beneath me tighter as his tongue licks down to my opening, licking up more of my juices as he goes.

"Oh!" I gasp as his tongue wiggles into my snug hole just a little bit.

"So tight. Gonna have to loosen you up," he murmurs, and I nod desperately.

"I need you," I beg, and he runs a finger between my folds, the digit swirling over my clit and driving me wild. "Please, Kip," I pant. "Don't tease me."

I love seeing this confident side of him: how he's taking control, how needy he seems to be to have me, and how he looks and touches me like I'm something precious.

We lock eyes and stare at each other as he slowly works one thick finger into me. I wince at the sharp string of pressure as he stretches me and he swallows hard.

"Are you a virgin, baby?" He asks, his voice low and guttural.

I nod silently, and he closes his eyes for a moment.

"Were you saving yourself for me?" He croaks, and I nod again. "Thank fuck. I was waiting for you too, baby."

I want to ask if that means that he's a virgin, too, but before I can, his mouth is back on me, and I forget about everything else.

His mouth loves my clit while he adds another finger, stretching my pussy wider. He works them in and out of me slowly, and a pressure starts to build low in my stomach, coiling tighter and tighter until it snaps.

"Kip!" I cry out as I fall over the edge, riding his fingers as my orgasm flows through me.

"Fuck, that was so fucking hot," he groans, and I look down to see him licking his fingers clean.

I sit up, intending to return the favor, but before I can, Kip grabs me and moves me to the center of the bed. He strips quickly, and I can only stare at his perfect body as he joins me in the middle of the bed.

"Sorry. It's not pretty to look at," he whispers, and I blink, looking up at him with confusion.

"What?" I ask, and he looks away from me.

"The scars," he says, and I blink, taking him in again.

"These?" I whisper, my fingers stroking over the raised red lines on his face, down his neck, and down his chest to his shoulder.

"Yeah," he chokes out.

My fingers trail lower to the other scars and bumps on his hip, and I look up at him.

"Bullets and an IED," he tells me without me having to ask.

"I'm sorry that you went through that," I whisper, leaning forward and pressing a kiss to one scar and then the next, and then the next.

"Ginger," he says, and I can hear the doubt in his voice.

I'm no stranger to being self-conscious. I've always been a bigger girl, and I've had to work to be confident in my own skin.

"I love your body. You look like a warrior. You *are* a warrior," I tell him as I continue to trail kisses across the scars. "Look at how strong you are. How brave."

I kiss lower, pushing him onto his back as I settle between his thighs. His cock is hard and resting against his flat stomach, and I place a kiss next to his belly button.

He sucks in a sharp breath, and I smile up at him as I wrap my hands around his dick.

"I might not be good at this," I warn him.

"You're doing amazing already," he says hoarsely, and I smile.

"I'm not really doing anything," I point out and he swallows hard.

"You're sitting next to me, naked, with your hand on my cock. I'm about two seconds from coming," he says, and it's the biggest ego boost that I've ever gotten.

"Have you thought about me, about us, doing this before?" I ask him as I lean down and swipe my tongue over the tip of his cock, licking up the drop of precum there.

"Only every single day for the past year."

"And what do I do in these fantasies?" I ask him as I trail my tongue down the underside of his cock.

"Fuck, Ginger," he groans, and I grin.

"Uh huh, but *how* do we fuck?" I ask him, and he stares down at me with fierce eyes.

"Every way. There's not a single thing that we haven't done in my head," he tells me, and I nod.

"You'll have to make a list so that we can get to all of it."

"A... list?" He asks, his eyes going hazy as I wrap my lips around him and start to suck his cock.

"Hmm," I hum around him, and his thighs tense.

"Fuck," he grits out, his hand coming up to tangle in my dark red hair.

I take more of him, all of the way until he bumps against the back of my throat. His length is starting to swell on my tongue already, and I swallow around him, wanting to taste his release.

"Ginger...baby...," he pants, and I wrap my hand around the length that I can't get in my mouth, working him in time with my mouth. "Ginger. Ginger!" He shouts, his hand tightening in my hair.

A moment later, his salty release coats my tongue, and I hurry to swallow it all down. I sit back on my heels and watch him as he catches his breath. Finally, he opens his eyes and looks right at me.

"I love you."

He says it so fiercely, and I nod. This man loves me with every fiber of his being. And I love him.

"I know. I love you too. Now make me yours."

He moves, rolling me under him, and I spread my legs wider for him, offering him all of me.

"You've been mine since you stepped foot in this town. You'll always be mine," he tells me as he starts to push into me.

"Yours," I agree, my body already starting to race for my release as he slowly bottoms out inside of me.

I don't even feel when he takes my virginity. All I can feel is his love for me. All I can focus on is him.

He kisses me, his hands on my breast, in my hair. It's like he can't stop touching me, even as he makes love to me. I wrap my legs around his waist, clinging to him as my orgasm brews inside of me. He kisses me, whispers that he loves me and I come undone.

"Kip!" I scream as I come, and he groans my name as he follows me over the edge.

I'm not sure when he moves, but a moment later, we're lying on our sides facing each other, both of us still panting and flushed.

"So that's one fantasy," I tell him and he huffs out a laugh.

"One down. A million more to go," he whispers, and I smile as I cuddle into his side.

I just need to close my eyes for a moment. That's what I tell myself as I nestle against him and slowly let sleep claim me.

I feel Kip kiss my forehead right before I drift off.

"Merry Christmas, Ginger," he whispers, and I smile as I fall asleep.

NINE

Kip

"SO IT GOES OLIVE, then Maple, then Saffron, and you're the baby," I clarify, and she nods against my chest. "Did you like being the baby?"

"Yeah, I just wish that... I had more time with them," she finishes softly, and I know that she's talking about her parents.

"I know, baby. I'm sorry."

"What about you? Ever wish that you had siblings?"

"Sometimes. It was lonely growing up with two doctors for parents. They were always too busy off saving other people to remember me, and then I would feel guilty for wishing that they were with me when I knew that their patients needed them."

"You needed them, too," she reminds me, and I nod.

"Yeah."

"Do you ever talk to them?"

"Sometimes, but not a lot. They're disappointed in me. They wanted me to be a doctor too, but I couldn't. It's not what I wanted."

"I couldn't do it either. All of the blood and stuff," she says with a shudder, and I smile.

"What do you want to do?" I ask her as I rub her back lazily with my fingers.

"I don't know. I just... I always wanted to be a mom. I want a family. I want a home."

"I'll give you that," I promise her, and she smiles up at me.

"I know you will."

She kisses my chest, and I smile. I could stay like this with her forever.

"We should get up," Ginger whispers, and I tighten my arms around her.

We've been lying in bed and cuddling, talking about anything and everything for the last few hours, and I don't want it to stop. I love being with her like this. It feels so right, so natural, and effortless.

"Five more minutes," I argue, and she laughs.

"We're going to be late if we stay in bed any longer."

I groan as she pulls away from me and watch as she stands and heads towards the bathroom.

"Come on. I'll let you wash my back," she says with a wink, and I grin.

"Anything else you want me to wash?" I ask, and she giggles as she heads into my bathroom.

She invited me and Huxley to spend Christmas with her family and friends, and we're due to be at her eldest sister, Olive's, house in an hour. I'm nervous to be around so many people, but Ginger is so excited, and I know that I'll have to get used to it. These people are going to be my in-laws, my family, soon. Very soon, if I get my way.

I step into the bathroom after Ginger, watching as she turns on the shower, and she smiles at me in the mirror, giving me an idea.

"Eyes on me, baby," I tell her, my voice low and filled with promise.

Her breathing shallows, and she watches me excitedly as I step up behind her. I keep my eyes locked on hers until her ass squirms against me. Then I grin wickedly and let my eyes drop, taking in all of her sexy curves.

She's so perfect. Every inch of her is like a work of art.

Normally, I would be self-conscious to have my scars on full display, but with Ginger, I forget all about them. She makes me feel handsome, like I'm the sexiest man alive. She makes me see my scars in a new light.

"Spread your legs," I order, and she hurries to widen her stance. "Wider," I growl, and a crimson blush spreads from her face down to her full tits.

I can see how turned on she is before I even look between her legs.

"You're soaked for me, baby. Does someone need their man to give them a nice good fuck?" I ask her, and she nods eagerly.

"Kip," she gasps as my cock brushes against her drenched folds.

"Hmm?" I hum as I reach up, my hands cupping her breasts, feeling the weight of them in my palms.

"Please!" She begs, and I grin.

"Since you asked so nicely," I whisper against the shell of her ear, and she shivers against me, her eyes locked on me.

I grip her hips, jerking them back until I'm lined up with her tight opening. We lock eyes once again as I slowly start to sink into her, my hands gripping her hips tightly as inch after inch slowly stretches her pussy.

"Fucking dripping for me," I groan, and she nods, her breaths coming in short pants as I fill her completely.

She's so tight, and I let go of her hip, reaching around and finding her clit. As soon as my thumb starts to stroke that little button, Ginger gasps, her eyes darkening as her pussy clamps down on my length.

We stare at each other in the mirror, the glass starting to get foggy from the steam from the shower. I start to move in and out of her, when her phone rings.

"The party," she gasps, and I grunt in acknowledgment, my pace picking up.

My hips slam into her ass over and over again, driving both of us higher with each thrust. She's so damn tight, so wet and hot, and everything that I will ever need.

Ginger grips the bathroom counter tight as I pound into her. I can tell that she's close, and I am too, but I need her to come first.

"Give it to me, baby," I order, my thumb working her clit in tight circles.

She cries out my name, and I can't take it.

I pull out, spinning her around and lifting her onto the counter. Then I'm slamming into her in the next breath.

"Kip!" She screams, and I grip her legs, holding them open as I rut into her.

Her tits are bouncing with each thrust, and I grit my teeth, my eyes locking with hers as she starts to come. Her juices coat my cock, her walls tightening around me, forcing my own orgasm out of me.

"Fuck," I grit out, and she moans my name.

Steam fills the room as we catch our breath and she smiles at me.

"It keeps getting better and better," she tells me, and I nod.

"Always. Now, wrap your legs around my waist. I'm not done with you," I tell her as my hands cup her ass, and I lift her, carrying her under the hot spray of the shower.

"We're going to be late," she whispers against my mouth and I shake my head.

"I can multitask," I tell her, grabbing her shampoo and massaging it into her hair with one hand while the other keeps her on my cock.

She squirms against me, bouncing up and down slightly, and I plant my feet, giving her more leverage. It doesn't take long before we've both forgotten about the shampoo and shower.

Her back rests against the shower tile, and we make out like teenagers as I slide lazily in and out of her. My cock brushes over her clit, and she moans against me. I kiss down her neck, my lips wrapping around one stiff nipple and sucking it into my mouth. She pants above me, and the sound echoes off the walls of the shower. It's music to my ears.

"I love you, Ginger. More than anything," I whisper against her wet skin.

"I love you too."

Our lips find each other again, and our movements pick up. We move together perfectly and it doesn't take long before we're both reaching our peaks once again.

She sighs as I set her down on her feet, and I smile as I grab her body wash and start to rub it over her body until soap bubbles cover every inch of her.

"My turn," she says, doing the same to me, and I smile as her hands move over my body.

"Love you," I say as we step out, and I wrap her in a towel.

"Love you too."

We race to get dry and then to get dressed. We make a quick stop at Ginger's apartment to grab the gifts that she got for everyone and then make the short drive to Olive and Xavier's place.

"Ready?" She asks me, and I nod.

"Yeah, I'm ready."

We gather up the presents, and I pause, passing her the one that I got for her.

"For me?" She asks, delighted, and I smile.

"Yeah. Open it."

She tears at the wrapping paper, and I watch her face as she lifts the lid and looks inside.

"It's...paperwork?" She asks as she pulls out the papers.

"No...well, yeah, for right now. I got you a puppy."

She looks up at me in surprise and I smile.

"I've seen you with all of the dogs in town. You love them. I just... I thought... I—"

"Thank you!" She shouts, wrapping her arms around me so tightly that I almost can't breathe. "Thank you, thank you."

"Of course. I'd do anything to make you happy, Ginger."

"I can't have a dog in my apartment," she tells me and I grin.

"Guess you'll have to move in with me then."

"Oh yeah?" She asks with a wide smile.

"Yeah."

"We'll see," she says, but I can tell that she's in.

"Merry Christmas, Ginger."

"Merry Christmas, Kip. I love you."

"I love you too."

"Best Christmas ever," she says, and I can't help but agree.

It's our first Christmas together, and I intend to make every other one perfect.

TEN

Ginger

FIVE YEARS LATER...

FIVE YEARS. It's hard to believe that it's been five years since that Christmas when everything changed. Since I found out that my secret admirer—the man I'd been falling for in those letters—was Kip. Five years since that fateful kiss under the mistletoe that sealed my heart to his.

Now, here we are, five years later, and Christmas has become even more magical than it used to be.

I stand in the doorway of our cozy little house, watching the snow fall softly outside. The world is quiet, blanketed in white, and the Christmas lights twinkle in the trees lining our street. It's perfect—just like the life we've built together.

Kip is in the living room, decorating the tree with the same focus and intensity he puts into everything. He's carefully hanging ornaments, stepping back every now and then to make sure everything is in its right place. I can't help but smile as I watch him, remembering how far we've come from that first Christmas.

"Kip," I call softly, stepping into the room. "You're going to run out of branches if you keep hanging ornaments that close together."

He looks over his shoulder at me, a grin spreading across his face. "I'm just making sure it's perfect."

"It's already perfect," I say, crossing the room to stand beside him. I wrap my arms around his waist, resting my chin on his shoulder as we both look at the tree.

Five years ago, I never would have imagined we'd be here. But now, with the tree glowing warmly in front of us, the house filled with the smell of fresh pine and the faint sound of Christmas music playing in the background, I can't imagine my life any other way.

"It's beautiful," I murmur, my arms tightening around him.

He leans down, pressing a kiss to the top of my head. "Not as beautiful as you."

I laugh softly, rolling my eyes. "You've been saying that for years, you know."

"Because it's true," he says, turning in my arms so that we're face to face.

I look up at him, my heart swelling with love. There's still a part of me that's amazed by how far we've come, how lucky I am to have found someone like Kip. He's everything I've ever wanted, and more than I ever thought I deserved. Five years, and I'm still falling in love with him every single day.

Goldfish comes into the room, and I bend down to

scratch him behind the ears before he heads over to his dog bed in the corner.

Kip and I got married six months after we got together, in a small ceremony here in Wolf Valley. Then we spent two weeks in Hawaii, enjoying the sun and water and each other. Two weeks after we got back home, we found out that I was pregnant.

To say that it was a whirlwind would be an understatement, but Kip was so strong and supportive throughout it all. It made me fall in love with him even more.

Since then, we've had our son, moved into a bigger house, and grown the business. I started working with Kip and Huxley at their company, and I've been handling the admin work ever since.

"You know," Kip says, his voice soft, "I was thinking about that first Christmas, when I finally got the nerve to kiss you under the mistletoe."

I smile, remembering it as if it were yesterday. "You mean when I ran across the room and practically jumped into your arms?"

He chuckles, his eyes crinkling at the corners. "Yeah, that part. I still think about how scared I was that night, wondering if you'd actually want me after you found out I was the one writing those letters."

My smile widens, and I press a kiss to his jaw. "I wanted you more than anything."

"And now?" he asks, his voice playful but with a hint of seriousness beneath it.

"Now," I say, leaning up on my tiptoes to kiss him softly, "I still want you. Always."

His arms wrap around me, pulling me closer, and for a moment, we're lost in each other, the rest of the world fading away like it always does when we're together.

But then a sound breaks the silence—a tiny voice from the other side of the room.

"Mama! Dada!"

Kip and I both turn at the sound, and my heart swells as I see our little boy, Sawyer, standing by the fireplace, his wide green eyes sparkling with excitement. He's holding one of the Christmas ornaments in his small hands, his dark hair a messy mop on his head.

"Look!" Sawyer says, holding up the ornament proudly.

I walk over, kneeling down in front of him as he shows me the ornament—a small wooden heart with the word *Love* carved into it. It's one of the first ornaments Kip and I ever bought together, back when we were just starting out, before our lives got filled with all the little moments and memories that now decorate our tree.

"Do you want to put it on the tree?" I ask, smiling at him.

Sawyer nods enthusiastically, his face lighting up with excitement. I stand up and help him reach one of the branches near the bottom of the tree, and he carefully hangs the ornament in place, his little face serious with concentration.

"Tada!" he says proudly.

"It's perfect!" I compliment him.

Kip walks over, ruffling Sawyer's hair with a grin. "You're right, buddy. It's perfect."

I step back, watching the two of them, and my heart feels like it might burst. This is our life now—our little family, our home filled with warmth and love, and it's more than I ever could have dreamed of.

The doorbell rings, and Sawyer's eyes widen with excitement. "Is it Santa?" he asks, bouncing on his toes.

I laugh, shaking my head. "No, sweetheart, it's probably Aunt Cora and Uncle Huxley."

Sawyer's face lights up even more at the mention of his favorite aunt and uncle, and he races toward the door, his little feet barely touching the ground as he runs.

I glance at Kip, who's grinning as he watches Sawyer disappear down the hallway. "You know, five years ago, I wouldn't have imagined us here," I say softly.

Kip turns to me, his expression softening. "Yeah. It's crazy to think about how much has changed."

I nod, my gaze drifting back to the tree, the soft glow of the lights casting a warm, golden hue over the room. "I didn't think I'd ever find this—find *you*—and now I can't imagine life without it."

Kip steps closer, wrapping his arms around me from behind. "I couldn't imagine it either."

I smile, leaning back against him as we stand there, soaking in the quiet of the moment.

The door opens, and I hear the familiar sound of laughter as Cora and Huxley step inside, Sawyer's excited voice echoing through the house as he tells them all about the tree and the ornaments he helped hang.

"Merry Christmas!" Cora calls out as she walks into the living room, her arms full of gifts, her face glowing with happiness.

"Merry Christmas," I reply, stepping forward to give her a hug. "You're just in time."

Huxley grins, clapping Kip on the back. "This place looks amazing. You guys went all out this year."

Kip chuckles. "Well, you know Ginger. She doesn't do anything halfway when it comes to Christmas."

I smile, shaking my head at him as I help Cora with the

gifts. It's true—I've always loved Christmas, and ever since Kip and I started this tradition of decorating together, it's become even more special. Especially now that we get to share it with Sawyer and our friends.

The evening passes in a blur of laughter and warmth, the house filled with the sound of music and the smell of gingerbread cookies baking in the oven. Sawyer is bouncing around, showing off the decorations to Cora and Huxley, while Kip and I steal quiet glances at each other, little moments of connection that remind me how lucky I am.

As the night winds down, and the house falls into a comfortable silence, I find myself standing by the window, watching the snow fall gently outside. The world is peaceful, and my heart feels full.

Kip walks up behind me, his arms wrapping around my waist as he rests his chin on my shoulder. "You okay?"

I nod, leaning back into him. "Yeah. I'm more than okay."

We stand there for a while, watching the snow, and I think about how far we've come, how much has changed. Five years ago, I was standing under the mistletoe, waiting for Kip to show up, nervous and unsure of what the future would bring.

Now, as I stand here with him, with our son asleep upstairs and our friends gathered in the warmth of our home, I know that I've found everything I've ever wanted.

"I love you," Kip whispers, his breath warm against my neck.

I smile, turning in his arms to face him. "I love you too."

And as we kiss, the snow falling softly outside, the lights twinkling around us, I know one thing for sure—this is the Christmas I'll remember for the rest of my life.

Because this is *our* Christmas. Our family. Our love. And it's perfect.

Want more of Kip and Ginger? Then be sure to check out this bonus scene of the night that their son, Sawyer, is born!

WANT A FREE BOOK?

You can grab Sweets **Here.**
**Check out my website, www.shawhart.com for
more free books!**

ABOUT THE AUTHOR

CONNECT WITH ME!

If you enjoyed this story, please consider leaving a review on Amazon or any other reader site or blog that you like. Don't forget to recommend it to your other reader friends.

If you want to chat with me, please consider joining my VIP list or connecting with me on one of my Social Media platforms. I love talking with each of my readers. Links below!

Website
Newsletter

A Very Mountain Man New Year

<u>Folklore</u>

<u>Kidnapping His Forever</u>

<u>Claiming His Forever</u>

<u>Finding His Forever</u>

<u>Rescuing His Forever</u>

<u>Chasing His Forever</u>

<u>Folklore: The Complete Series</u>

<u>Holiday Hearts</u>

Be Mine

Falling in Love

Holly Jolly Holidays

<u>Love Notes</u>

<u>Signing Off With Love</u>

<u>Care Package Love</u>

<u>Wrong Number, Right Love</u>

<u>Kings Gym</u>

Fighting Fire With Fire

Fighting Tooth and Nail

Fighting Back From Hell

<u>Mine To</u>

<u>Mine to Love</u>

<u>Mine to Protect</u>

<u>Mine to Cherish</u>

<u>Mine to Keep</u>

Mine to: The Complete Series

<u>Sequoia: Stud Farm</u>

Branded

Bucked

Roped

Spurred

<u>Sequoia: Fast Love Racing</u>

Jump Start

Pit Stop

Home Stretch

<u>Telltale Heart</u>

<u>Bought and Paid For</u>

<u>His Miracle</u>

<u>Pretty Girl</u>

<u>Telltale Hearts Boxset</u>

ALSO BY SHAW HART

Still in the mood for Christmas books?

Stuffing Her Stocking, Mistletoe Kisses, Snowed in For Christmas, Coming Down Her Chimney

Love holiday books? Check out these!

For Better or Worse, Riding His Broomstick, Thankful for His FAKE Girlfriend, His New Year Resolution, Hop Stuff, Taming Her Beast, Hungry For Dash, His Firework

Looking for some OTT love stories?

Her Scottish Savior, Baby Mama, Tempted By My Roommate, Blame It On The Rum, Wild Ride, Always

Looking for a celebrity love story?

Bedroom Eyes, Seducing Archer, Finding Their Rhythm

In the mood for some young love books?

Study Dates, His Forever, My Girl

Some other books by Shaw:

The Billionaire's Bet, Her Guardian Angel, Falling Again, Stealing Her, Dreamboat, Making Her His, Trouble

www.ingramcontent.com/pod-product-compliance
Lightning Source LLC
Chambersburg PA
CBHW061354160726
47995CB00001B/314